I LOVE MY NATURAL HAIR

WRITTEN BY
BRIANA WILLIAMSON
MATNIQUE WILLIAMSON
MYA WILLIAMSON

ILLUSTRATED BY CAMERON WILSON

This project is dedicated to The Ivory Tour. This project would not have come together without the opportunity to attend The Ivory Tour as a family. Thank you Tobe, Fat, Nell and Black Angels for helping to affirm that beauty still exists in the natural form.

THIS BOOK BELONGS TO:

_____

I love my natural hair, it's so **PRETTY** and **FREE**.

I love my natural hair,
As **KINKY** and **CURLY** as can be.

I love my natural hair, so **DIFFERENT** and **UNIQUE**.

I love my natural hair, it's so **CUTE** and so **CHIC**.

I love my natural hair,
how it shimmers and **SHINES**.

I love my natural hair,
with my curls loose or defined!

I love my natural hair, because my hair is my **CROWN.**

The End.

Made in the USA
Monee, IL
04 July 2022